# Dalmatian in a DIGGER

by
Rebecca Elliott

DUGGER DUGGER DIGGER
What's that noise?
DUGGER DUGGER DIGGER
It woke me up!

# Dalmatian in a DIGGER!

DUGGER
DUGGER
DIGGER

He's scooping up dirt.

He's dumping it over there.

DUGGER DUGGER DIGGER

BRMMM
BRMMM WHEEE

What's THAT noise?

BRMMM BRMMM WHEEE

It really made me jump!

BRMMM
BRMMM
WHEEE

Oh my! It's a . . .

Camel in a CRANE!

BRMMM BRMMM WHEEE

She's picking up the logs.

Then lifting them up high.

BRMMM BRMMM WHEEE

DUMP SPLAT CRASH

What's THAT noise?

DUMP SPLAT CRASH

It sounds really messy!

DUMP SPLAT CRASH

Oh my! It's a . . .

Duck
in a
DUMP
TRUCK!

He's filling up
his truck.

He's delivering
the dirt.

DUMP
-SPLAT-
CRASH

I love
dump trucks!

TUG TUG BEEP
Now what's THAT noise?

TUG TUG BEEP
It sounds really BIG!

TUG TUG BEEP

Oh my! It's a . . .

# Bear
## in a
# BULLDOZER!

He's pushing all the rocks.

**TUG TUG BEEP**

He's making a huge pile.

**TUG TUG BEEP**

I love bulldozers!

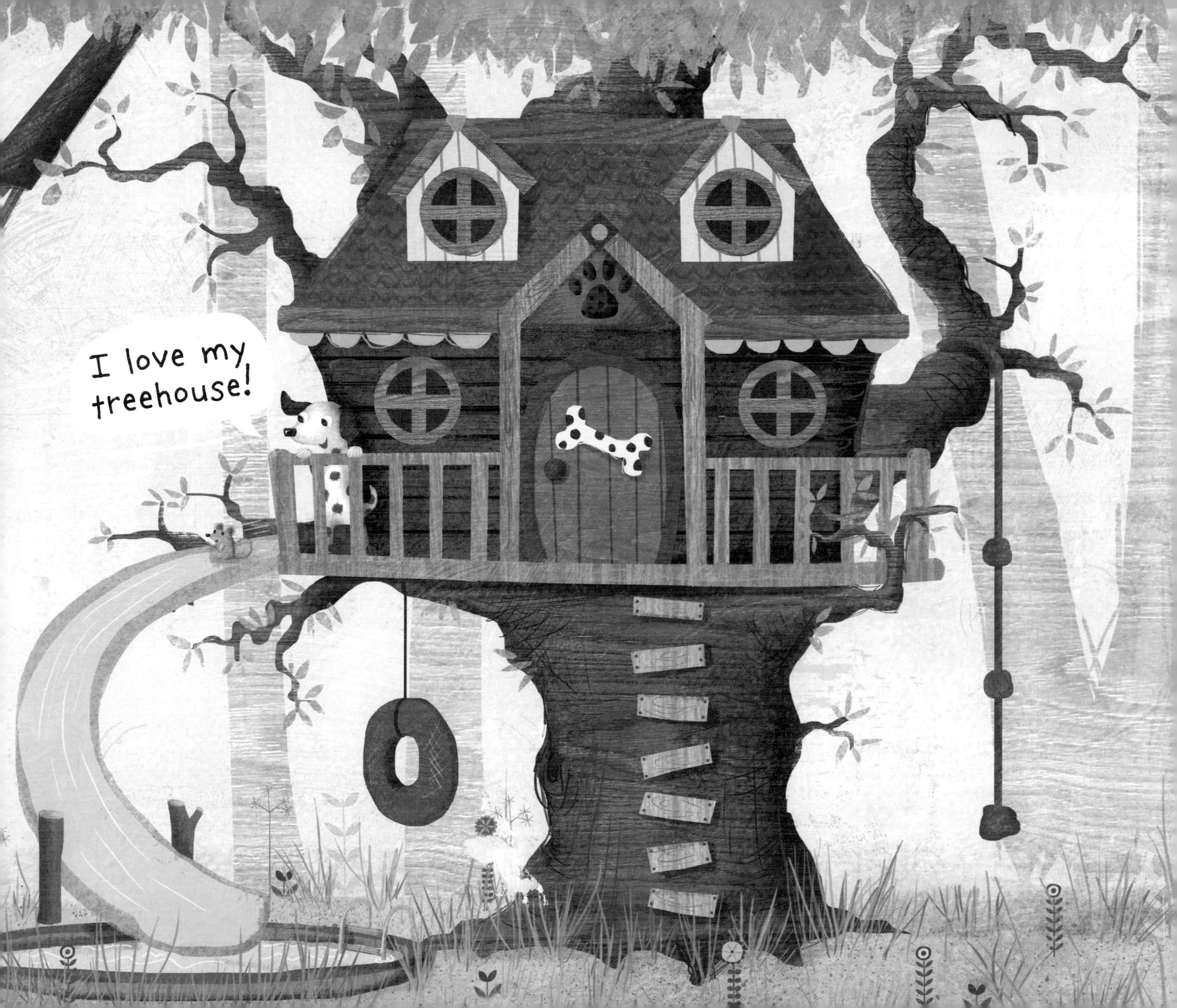
I love my treehouse!

For Tom and Oli. May you never be too old for dogs and diggers. — R.E.

Raintree is an imprint of Capstone Global Library Limited, a company incorporated in England and Wales having its registered office at 264 Banbury Road, Oxford, OX2 7DY – Registered company number: 6695582

www.raintree.co.uk
myorders@raintree.co.uk

Copyright © 2017 Rebecca Elliott
The author's moral rights are hereby asserted.

Illustrations by Rebecca Elliott

ISBN 978 1 78202 596 2 (hardcover)
ISBN 978 1 4747 8252 4 (paperback)

23 22 21 20 19
10 9 8 7 6 5 4 3 2 1

A CIP catalogue for this book is available from the British Library.

Designer: Lori Bye

Printed and bound in India.

Hi! I'm Little Mouse. I'm Dalmatian's best friend. Can you spot me throughout the book?